The Devil In Me

The Devil In Me

Copyright © K.I. Lynn

Cover image licensed by shutterstock.com/ ©pudi studio
Cover design by L.J. Anderson

Editors
Marti Lynch
N Isabelle Blanco

Publication Date: May 5, 2014
Genre: FICTION/Romance/Erotica
Copyright © 2014 K.I. Lynn
All rights reserved

Chapter 1

Lying on the bed of my childhood room should have been a nostalgic experience. Instead, I stared up at the ceiling, boxes in my periphery and the alarm blaring next to me.

What the fuck happened?

I rubbed my face, then swung my legs over the edge of the bed, slamming my hand down on the alarm as I stood. There was very little room to maneuver around the already small room, but I'd already filled up the basement and half the garage with all the shit I'd accumulated in my life. I cursed when I slammed my toe into the wheel of the suitcase on the floor, giving it a swift kick before grabbing some clothes out of it.

The house remained quiet as I made my way to the bathroom. I sighed as I looked down at the boner curving my cock up. Pissing with one annoyed the crap out of me, but had become a daily thing since sex for me was non-existent lately.

Once I threw on the random jeans and shirt I'd grabbed, forgoing styling my hair for now and doing the basic morning routine, I headed downstairs. The smell of coffee perked me up a little, and I grabbed a cup as I made a quick bowl of oatmeal before finding my mom sitting in the living room.

"Morning." I kissed her forehead and sat down on the couch, placing the oatmeal in front of her.

She smiled at me, and the sight depressed me, but I tried not to show it. Her face had become a shade of sickly yellow, there were dark circles under her eyes, and every bit of her hair was gone. I hardly recognized her as the woman I'd known my entire life.

"Good morning, sweetie."

"How are you feeling?" I reached forward and grabbed the multiple pill bottles sitting on the coffee table.

"Like I've been hit by a truck."

I dished out the four pills for her morning dosage and handed them to her along with some water. Her face scrunched up.

"Jared, I don't think…"

"Mom, don't fight me on this. Not again."

"I'm nauseous."

"And one of these will help with that, but you have to get it and that oatmeal in you." I handed her the bowl and stared at her as she took a tentative bite.

She'd lost her appetite with all the treatments and drugs. The biggest fear I had was of her giving up. I wasn't about to let that happen, especially not with my sister pregnant.

"I have some clients at one, but I'll be home by five. Cassie's off today. She has a doctor's appointment this morning, and then she'll be by."

She narrowed her eyes at me. "I'm fine by myself, you know. I'm not an invalid."

I stood up and grabbed the phone, setting it on the table next to her. "No, you're not, but this is always the rough day. I'll be back soon."

Her expression dropped—a contrast to her words. She didn't really want to be alone, no matter what she said. "Where are you going? I thought you didn't have to work until this afternoon."

"Just running an errand. I'll be back soon." I picked up her Kindle from across the room and set it next to the phone. "Read something today. TV will rot your brain." I winked at her.

She rolled her eyes and swatted at me. "Get out of here, stinker."

I beamed at her and headed out the door and onto the street. The sun was shining, birds were singing, and a warm breeze blew—

About fucking time. It'd been the longest winter in my thirty-one years.

It was a great day for a walk down to St. Joan of Arc, a Catholic church a few blocks from the 1920s cottage, in a historic neighborhood of Indianapolis, my parents purchased over thirty years ago. My parents were raised in two different religions, so we didn't go to church that often—about once a month—but Joan of Arc was one of the more steady locations. I believed in God. Period. So, what did it matter what church I visited to talk to Him?

Stepping into the church felt a little odd—it'd been years since I'd been within its walls. The cumbersome weight of my head and heart slowed my walk down the aisle. I

~ 3 ~

slipped into a pew about halfway down and folded my hands together. The place was empty.

"Hey, big man." I sighed and fidgeted with my hands. "I know I'm not good at visiting, and I should come more often. People stare when I do, always assuming, but you know the truth." I leaned forward, resting my arms on the back of the pew in front of me. "I have to ask—are you testing me? Because if you are, did you have to throw so much at me at once?"

I stared up at the altar, lit up by the sun shining through the stained glass windows all over the stone structure. No response to my question came—not that I expected one.

"I can deal with all of it, but Mom…" I took a deep breath, trying not to let her condition get to me. "Cassie was a wreck when she found out about the cancer. You took Dad three years ago, and I'm not sure Mom has the strength to fight this. She's still heartbroken."

I leaned back, my gaze tracing over Jesus on the cross, and got lost in my own head. In the time I sat there, still as a statue, a few people came and went. I didn't look at them, but I felt their eyes on me as they passed. Most thought I worshiped the Devil or some shit like that because of the way I looked. Tattoos covered a lot of my skin, and my jet black hair, often in a short mohawk, gave off a taboo vibe to most of the church-going folk.

I could admit it—I had a nice body. Being a personal trainer meant I had to be able to do everything I put my clients through.

The nerves on my neck lit up, tingling down my side. It woke me from my trance, and I turned to find innocent eyes looking at me from one row up on the other side of the aisle. When our gazes connected, she didn't flinch, her eyes didn't widen, but a slight blush did appear on her cheeks.

The strange current continued to move through me.

I was caught, roped in, staring at her.

She seemed young—early twenties maybe. I went from studying Jesus to studying the woman who called to me. That was the only way I could explain the firing off of every nerve ending in my body.

She had large, blue doe eyes that bored into my soul. Dark brown, wavy hair curled around her smooth, pale skin and full cheeks. She nabbed her full bottom lip with her teeth before looking away, hiding from me.

It didn't stop me from staring at her. I tilted my head to the side, forehead scrunched as I tried to figure out what the hell had just happened—and why my cock was so hard. It was just a look, but at the same time, it felt like so much more. A connection, and not that love-at-first-sight bullshit.

Base level between a man and a woman—a need that populated the earth.

Our strange interaction caused images to course through my mind of fucking her on the altar. Was she as untouched as her innocent face suggested? She looked soft, inviting, and corruptible. How would her full hips feel beneath my hands as I thrust my cock into her?

I turned back to the front and began to ask for forgiveness for the sinful things I was thinking about doing to her. My dick, however, continued to dream. A small groan slipped from my lips, and her head snapped up. I cupped my cock through my jeans, adjusting it so it didn't press so hard against the seam. It twitched against my palm as she squirmed in her seat.

Fuck.

I sat still, staring at her profile. Her lips parted, skin pink, and she moved her ass again. I blew out a breath to calm myself. It was ridiculous. I was just horny because I hadn't had sex since Monica gave me a break-up fuck three months prior.

After a few minutes, she stood and headed to the confessional. I couldn't help but turn to look at her delectable ass as she walked. Soft curves called to me, begging me to touch them, own them.

As soon as she stepped out of sight, I ran down the steps to the restroom and locked myself in. I splashed some water on my face, staring at the image in front of me. Someone else stared back. My brown eyes were almost black, lids heavy with a force of lust I'd never experienced.

My teeth clenched, muscles coiled tight as my hips rocked, searching for her. I grabbed hold of the sink, my breath heavy and hard.

What is wrong with me?

It was overpowering. An internal battle for control waged as consuming need pumped through my veins. I popped open my jeans and pulled out my cock. It didn't matter that I stood in the bathroom of a church—I had to get off before I went insane.

I shuddered as I wrapped my hand around my hard dick, the force almost sending me to the ground. It throbbed, overly sensitive, and I had a hard time keeping my focus on the task with each intense stroke. My imagination went wild with thoughts of touching her, of pulling her out of the confessional and bending her over a pew.

I wanted her with a primal intensity that consumed me. Fuck her raw. Make her need me as much as I was suddenly dying for her. I wanted to hear her screams bouncing off the stone walls, mark her with my come. Taint her innocence, then fuck her all over again.

A roar ripped through me, every muscle strained to the limit. My balls were tight, and with a few hard tugs, I exploded all over the mirror and sink. I couldn't stop coming, my body jerking hard with each spurt.

My legs gave out, and I sprawled out onto the floor, trying to breathe again. Come continued to drip out of my dick.

Once again, I found myself staring at a ceiling, wondering what the fuck happened.

Chapter 2

A few hours later, I was in the gym, working out one of my clients and trying not to think of what happened earlier.

"Come on, Teri." I held the sparring mitts up. "One, two, one, elbow, knee, roundhouse."

She took a moment to catch her breath, then swung forward. The combination was repetitious, ten each side, her hits pounding in tandem with the blood pulsing through me.

My mind wandered back to this morning. I'd stayed on the bathroom floor of the church for a few minutes before sneaking out and back home. Mom was asleep, and I rushed upstairs, still confused as to what came over me. The feeling followed me home, and I busted another nut before heading to work.

I pushed my client more than normal, taking my confusion out on her with a wicked tough session. She wasn't the most coordinated, but she enjoyed the boxing.

"Good workout." I gave her a high five after pulling the gloves off her.

"You were mean today!" She lightly punched my shoulder and laughed.

I shrugged and smirked. "No pain, no gain."

A little while later, I stopped in the break room for a drink, my last client gone for the day, and took a moment to decide if I wanted to work out on my own. Maybe that would calm my ass down. I scanned the room, head tilted back as I drank, and my eyes landed on a poster showcasing a woman's before and after fitness program pictures. She had brown hair similar to the girl I'd seen, and soft curves. My dick twitched.

"Dude, you need to stop moping. You're scaring the girls away with your brooding." Dex reached into the fridge, pulling out a water before coming to stand by me and elbowing me in the arm.

"Sorry, man, it's just…" I blew out a sigh. My eye caught a flyer for a boxing class on Thursday nights, one I knew nothing about, and it wasn't me teaching it. "Fucking bitch!" I slammed my hand into the corkboard, knocking it off the wall and onto the floor.

Dex stepped back. "Yo, you need to cool it."

"Did you know about this?"

"About what?"

I picked up the flyer and shoved it at him. His eyes widened. "Holy shit! She's lost her fucking mind. I bet it's that shithead Shone. I saw them getting cozy the other day." He shook his head. "Sorry."

I began pacing the wall. "I don't fucking care if that slut is banging that prissy asshole. I'm the resident boxing trainer. *I* teach all the classes."

"Who's the prissy one?" Monica called from the doorway.

I froze and slowly spun toward her. My stomach turned, and I questioned why I'd ever been attracted to her—fake blonde hair, fake nails, fake tan, overdone makeup, and a fake personality. Even her once-womanly body was gone, replaced with too many muscles. No softness in her at all. The transformation had occurred over the last two years. She no longer resembled the girl of six years prior.

"I see there's a new class." My jaw clenched. It wasn't the first time in recent weeks she'd done something that set me off.

One of her drawn-on brows quirked up. "Yes, there is."

"And some shithole who's been here for less than six months is teaching it?"

"New blood."

"New blood?" I stepped forward, looming over her. "I fucking started the program. I teach every class."

"And now there's someone to take some of the stress off you, especially with your mom's condition."

My eyes grew wide. "Don't you fucking bring her up. This is about you being a raging bitch, for bitch's sake. Which I don't get, because you were the one who cheated on me and flaunted that shit in my face."

She put her hand on my chest and ran it across my shoulder. I wanted to throw up.

"Ooh, I like this side of you, Jared. Are you jealous I'm sucking someone else's cock now?"

"Go fuck yourself." I snarled and pushed past her, heading to the locker room to get my crap. I needed to get the fuck out of what once had been my second home but now felt like my prison.

I slammed my fist against the metal door of my locker, cursing, not even noticing that Dex followed me.

"What the fuck is up with you?" He sat down on the bench behind me. "We've been friends for years, but I've never seen you blow up like that. I mean, I know you're pissed at her, and she's doing everything she can to push you out of here and sign over your part of the business, but still."

I shook my head. "I don't know. I really fucking don't."

"I think you do, and it's not about her or your mom, so spill."

"Those two have caused a lot of stress." I looked around the room, making sure none of Monica's snoops were within listening distance. "I can't stop thinking about this girl I saw this morning."

He stared at me for a moment before leaning over and laughing. "That's *not* what I expected you to say!" He wiped away a tear from laughing so hard, which pissed me off more. "Dude, you need to get your dick wet. Take out some of your stress on a pussy."

My eyes widened, and I stared at him. Something inside me rumbled, those scenes I'd imagined flying through my mind. Fuck, I wanted some girl I didn't even know and would probably never see again. It was so strong that I didn't want to just get in and get off. I wanted to decimate her to where nothing else mattered but her pussy wrapped around me.

"Shit, man, put the snake away!"

I looked down and sighed, adjusting my new hard-on. "Told you." I pulled my bag out and grabbed my keys. "Is it a bad sign that a cardinal sin has taken control of me?"

~ 11 ~

Dex sighed. "I think you're just going through a lot of crap and need a release. Let's go out tomorrow night, get a few drinks and relax."

"It's Mom's rough days."

"Then see if Cass can help."

I nodded. "I'll call you later."

--oOo--

The next day, I was no closer to figuring out the lust I had for her, my mysterious torturer. I didn't even have a name to call out when I came. What I did have was a constantly hard dick and a grumpy attitude. All because a girl looked at me.

I'd lost my fucking mind.

Was it really that I hadn't had sex in a while? Or was it the stress of my mom's illness coupled with Monica screwing me over?

Six fucking years I wasted with her. I should've ended it, seen the writing on the wall long before finding out she'd been cheating on me. Instead, I was too busy looking at expanding our company and taking care of my mom.

"Oh, J, your lawyer called for you earlier."

I stopped in my tracks to stare back at my little sister. "And you're just telling me now as I'm walking out the door?"

She shrugged and ran a hand over her baby bump. "I'll say it was pregnant brain."

That got me to smile and shake my head. "What time did he call?"

"Right before you got home." She pulled on her ponytail of jet-black hair that matched mine and tilted her head in that curious way she'd done her whole life. "What's going on?"

"Exploring options to get away from Monica."

She nodded. "Good. That bitch needs to go down."

"I thought you liked her." I peeked over to look at Mom's snoozing silhouette.

"I did, but then she fucked with my brother. Honestly, she turned into someone else over the last few years. I couldn't relate to her anymore."

"You and me both."

It was true. Cassie and Monica had been close in the beginning. Back then, they were a lot alike. When Cassie opened up her gourmet pet store, I thought she was crazy. Three years later, she had a booming business, married one of her customers, and was happier than I'd ever seen her.

I pulled open the door, but didn't get my foot over the threshold before she called me back. She padded into the entryway. "Give me a call if you need a lift, okay?"

I leaned forward and kissed her cheek. "Will do."

A short drive later, I parked my truck in back of the restaurant right next to Dex's.

As soon as I entered through the back door, eyes landed on me. Granted, if I'd walked into some place in Carmel, it would've been worse, but at Union Jack's, in the heart of Broad Ripple, only my muscles made me stand out.

Not that I normally minded the attention. After all, I covered my skin with art and had a hot body. My full sleeves were highly visible with the short-sleeved shirt I had on.

My problem today was how fucked up I'd been lately. I didn't want to deal with curious eyes and stupid chicks looking to hook up with a bad boy.

I found Dex at the bar and hopped onto the stool next to him. He cocked his head and pushed a bottle my way.

"Gonna be a few for a table."

"Always is."

Union Jack Pub had the best Chicago-style pizza in town. The downside? It took about an hour to cook. Then again, that left us lots of time for drinking, which I desperately needed.

The Reds were on one of the TVs and we sat in silence, watching the game and letting the alcohol work its magic. One or two minutes later, the pager went off, and we headed to the hostess stand. She led us to our seats, which were back in the bar area.

Fine by me—closer to the drinks.

My skin vibrated as we reentered the section, a shudder rolling down my back and through my legs before pulsing into my cock.

"Fuck me."

It was the same feeling. The one that hit me the moment she walked in the church and never left me. The one that haunted me. She was there. She had to be.

I scanned the room, my eyes transfixed on a curvy figure a few feet away as I slid into the booth seat, and everything slowed down. I began to wonder if I'd really lost it. My torturer from the church pews was parading around in barely-cover-her-ass shorts and a vest that pushed her tits up and out, begging for me to bite them.

I prayed for her to be our waitress. At the same time, I was scared—uncertain if I could control myself with her so close.

Dex waved his hand in front of me. "Yo, Jared, what the fuck? See something you like?" He followed my gaze.

"That's her." I couldn't tear my eyes away from the curve of her tits and ass.

"Her who?"

"The girl from the church."

"The waitress? That's the girl?" He glanced back at her. "Girl's got curves. Definitely different from Monica."

I rubbed my face and shook my head. "She could be so much trouble."

"Would it be worth it?"

"I'd probably end up in jail."

He held his beer up, then took a swig. "Go for it. Like I said, you need to damage a pussy."

Worst nightmare or heavenly dream, I didn't know, but she was headed right for us.

Chapter 3

"Hi, I'm Hope, and I'll be your waitress." Her voice was sweet and melodic, and I imagined it screaming my name. Her eyes scanned the table, a fake smile plastered on her face, but there was a flicker of recognition when her gaze landed on me.

Her breath hitched, pupils dilated, lips parting as I stared straight at her. The intense feelings that had taken all control at the church came surging back, and I gripped the edge of the table, jaw locked tight.

"Hello, Hope."

Her eyes fluttered as I said her name, and she no longer seemed to be able to stand still.

"Umm, our s-specials today are the turkey melt, clam chowder, and two-dollar draft beer." Her cheeks flushed. "Can I get you anything to drink?"

My cock got so hard, begging to be closer. What was it about her?

"You." I couldn't help myself. It was the truth.

Her eyes widened, and she nabbed her bottom lip between her teeth just as she'd done the other day.

Dex broke in, reminding us both where we were. "We have a tab going at the bar—can you get us a bucket of Dos Equis and some limes? That'd be great."

She blinked and looked at Dex, who was trying not to laugh. "Right, will do. Are you r-ready to order?"

"Not yet."

She stared, stuck for a moment. "Oh, okay, I'll just… I'll be back with the beer."

I couldn't take my eyes off her as she walked away, and I almost launched out of my seat when she looked back at me.

"Wow. What the fuck was that?"

I turned back to Dex and flexed my hands into fists, attempting to keep myself in place. "That's what I've been trying to figure out for days." I glanced back over at the bar where she collected our order.

"I'm beginning to believe your talk about deadly sins. You might die if you don't get your cock in that girl!"

My jaw clenched. "Not funny, man. I'm two dick pulses away from finding her and fucking her right now."

He held his hands up. "Sorry, sorry. You didn't see it from my perspective, though. Talk about intense."

"Let's change the subject."

"Okay… So, Monica?"

I twisted my head in an attempt to crack my neck. Even her name couldn't subdue the fire. It only ignited another kind—hatred.

"She's doing shit on purpose to piss me off. That boxing class isn't the beginning, and I don't see it being the end."

Even his face dropped. "Yeah. She's moved some of my clients as well. My girl is threatening my balls if I don't start bringing in more money."

An idea I'd been contemplating popped out of my mouth before I even thought about actually saying it. "If I leave, you're coming with me, right?"

My sudden topic switch stopped him mid-sip. "You thinking about opening your own place?"

The beer arrived, but I didn't even notice when someone brought it by because *she* didn't deliver it. I downed the one I was working on, then popped the top off the next. It was half gone in seconds.

Dex didn't say anything.

"Thinking. I can't do it now, but when my mom's better."

He grinned. "You're gonna decimate Monica, aren't you?"

I finished off the second and pulled out a third. "Yup. I get a large portion of the money from those classes. If she thinks I'm just going to let her push me out, she's very wrong."

"You practically built that place. Hell, I was your client when you opened."

I held my bottle up and smirked. "And look at you now."

After the third one on an empty stomach, I started to feel good, and my muscles relaxed. That was when she returned—my siren.

She avoided me, looking at Dex instead as he ordered us an appetizer and pizza—the same thing we ate every time. The intense reaction I had to her crashed over me like it had never waned with her farther away. It crippled me. Every muscle tensed to keep me in place.

If she looked at me, there would be no way to stop myself.

From what?

That was the million-dollar question. All answers involved her skin against mine in some capacity—the more, the dirtier, the better.

Her hand shook as she scribbled our order, eyes looking down as they rotated toward me. She didn't make it past the height of my chest before her lips parted and she stopped.

"The pizza will take about an hour, but I'll get the appetizer out shortly."

"Thank you, Hope." My voice was harsh, thick, my dick twitching when she licked her lips.

I had something for her to lick. In fact, it had her name and hers alone on it.

The thought stopped me cold. Realization took hold, my fever for her burning me from inside.

She had to be the one to get me off. Only *her* touch, *her* lips, *her* pussy would do. Until then, I would continue down my maddening spiral into hell, lust consuming me until there was nothing left but a devil bent on taking her.

"You're so fucked."

I leaned forward and slammed my head against the table. "I think I need some air."

"You need something, but air isn't gonna help you."

My eyes were glued to her as she moved around, noticing how she avoided looking in my direction. She recognized me from the church. Was she embarrassed?

~ 19 ~

Curiosity added to my already-insane attraction, and I wanted to know *why*.

Why was she avoiding me? Why did I need her so much? Why her?

Why couldn't I stop wanting her?

By beer six, an appetizer, a passed hour, and my obsession avoiding me, I was pissed in both the British and American sense. I batted the newest empty bottle around the tabletop until Dex's hand slapped down on it.

"We came here to drink, watch the game, and have a good time. Your moody, hyper sexed-up ass is fucking that up."

"We also came to take a load off."

"Not get a load off."

I flipped him the bird. "Keep it up, and you aren't coming with me. I'll leave your ass with the bitch and the prissy boy."

He smirked and passed me another beer. "Nah, you need me too much. I'm better looking."

"Hell, no."

"It's true. The girls at the gym did a poll." He flexed his muscles and grinned. Corn-fed Indiana farm boy with blond hair and blue eyes. Add in the body he spent too much time on and the tattoos, along with his ultra-friendly personality—he could be hotter than me. I'd never admit it to his ass though. It amazed me his girl put up with him.

"That's because you're always taking your shirt off and flirting with every female that walked in. Monica always got mad when I looked at another woman."

"I still won."

I shook my head. "I demand a recount."

A shudder rippled through me right before Hope arrived at our table with our pizza in hand.

"She'll settle this." I pointed to her, shocking her enough to look up at me.

Her fucking doe eyes were a gut punch. I imagined them looking up at me with her mouth around my cock.

Dex shook his head. "Yeah, she's not a good judge."

"What?"

"Huh?" Her brow scrunched up, lost to the conversation I'd thrust her into.

Mmm, thrust.

My hips flexed, and I fought the incredible urge to touch her, to lean forward and lick her skin. Losing my inhibitions with her around was a bad combination.

Dex turned to her. "We're having a debate on who's hotter, but I already know who you'll say."

Her brow scrunched, and a clarity I hadn't seen, moved through her. "What does that mean?"

"Are you going to tell me you'd say me after the eye-humping that's been going on between you two?"

Her mouth and eyes popped open as she stared at him. I wanted to give him shit for calling us out, but I'd become transfixed by her parted lips. The image of running my cock head against them before pushing into her hot mouth was squashed when she turned to me with an angry pout and attempted glare, then walked away.

"Thanks, man."

He dished out a piece of pizza, grinning as he eyed it. "Truth is tough sometimes. Just seeing if your little obsession can handle it."

I looked in the direction she went and sighed. "I don't know if she can handle me."

"There is that. You're gonna have to fuck her before you can get to know her."

I pulled a piece onto my plate and tossed some crushed red peppers on top. I sighed. "This didn't turn out to be the relaxing night I'd hoped for."

He tipped his head back and laughed. "That's 'cause your dick isn't being touched by that girl of yours."

My brow furrowed. "She's not mine."

"Yet." His smile fell, and he let out a hard breath. "In all seriousness, the chemistry is obvious. I wasn't kidding about you fucking her before seeing if there's something more permanent than the lust that's pouring out of you." He pulled the last beer out of the bucket and popped the top. "And instead of being the third bad thing to happen to you in such a short time, she could be the one good thing."

Two questions went through my mind with his comments. Was he right about a good thing, and was I capable of handling all of that?

A half hour later, I patted my overly stuffed stomach and had a nice buzz going on. I texted Cassie to pick me up in about thirty minutes. There was no way I was going to attempt to drive. I knew my limit, and I hit it two beers and four pieces of deep-dish pizza ago.

Hope remained scarce while we ate, and refused to even look at us when she dropped off the check. I blamed Dex for embarrassing her.

When she reached for my credit card, I grabbed her wrist and pulled her toward me to whisper in her ear. "I'll be back for you."

A blush spread on her face as she looked at me. She licked her lips as she pulled away.

I continued to stare at her, my body buzzing. "I am so fucked."

Chapter 4

The morning after seeing Hope at Union Jack's, I awoke just after eight with a small hangover and dried jizz all over my skin and clothes. The memory of masturbating while thinking about her was clear, but I must have fallen right to sleep after I came.

After a shower, I headed downstairs. Cassie and Mom were playing cards on the dining room table. I smiled, happy to see Mom looking perkier than she had over the last few days.

"Morning." Cassie smirked at me.

The devious tone in her voice set me on edge, and I narrowed my gaze at her before grunting in return. I poured a cup of coffee and grabbed a protein bar, then headed in to join the girls. Mom looked up at me, and I kissed her head as I walked around the table, making sure to ruffle up Cassie's hair as I moved to take a seat.

Cassie slapped at my hand, scowling up at me. "Be nice. I left my warm, comfy bed to come pick your drunk ass up last night."

"It wasn't that late." I peeked at the scorecard. The cards told me 500 Rummy, and the paper told me Mom was winning.

Go, Mom.

"No, but I was snuggled in bed with my husband."

"Oh, you were gettin' it on."

She shook her head while Mom's chuckle danced around the room. "So, you going to tell me about this girl?"

My brow scrunched up. "What girl?"

She rolled her eyes and set down a row of cards before discarding. "I had the unfortunate sight of a bulge in your pants when you got in the car." She made a yacking sound.

"Hmm, that. Well…it's complicated."

"Good to know your equipment still works." Mom didn't even look up from her cards as she muttered under her breath.

Cassie and I turned to her with what had to be matching looks of horror on our faces.

"Eww!"

"I…I don't know what to say to that, Mom. What the hell?"

She shrugged and laid down some cards, ending the hand. "Well, with what happened with Monica, I wondered if she might've given you something that made your wiener fall off."

Cassie howled with laughter, banging her hand on the table and giving no care to the fact that she'd just lost their game. I couldn't stop staring at my mother, who smiled as she tallied up their scores.

"And on that note, I'm outta here." Cassie slid her chair back and stood. She leaned over and punched my shoulder. "Tag."

I nodded and took a sip of my coffee. "Thanks, Cass."

She mussed up my hair, getting me back for earlier. I glared up at her. She was lucky I hadn't done anything with it yet.

"Later, cranky." She hugged Mom and kissed her cheek. "Darren and I will be over for dinner tomorrow night."

"All right."

She waved goodbye, and silence filled the room. Mom looked around the room for something to do.

"You up for another game?" I motioned to the cards.

She smiled and began shuffling. Guess I had my answer.

--oOo--

Thirty-six hours after seeing her, I still had Hope on the brain. It was accentuated by the three-mile trek back to the parking lot to get my truck. Luckily, Dex checked for me, and it was still there and not towed.

I spent the entire day before with Mom, and completely forgot to have Cassie drop me off on her way to work. After all, her store was a block down Broad Ripple Avenue from Union Jack's.

My attempt at running the distance was squashed by my hard dick trying to bounce around in my shorts. I should have put on some compression shorts instead of the boxer-briefs I wore. Hindsight was supposed to be twenty-twenty, but all I saw was Hope. I couldn't stop—thinking about her, wanting her, needing her, and desiring her. It was too much. I knew where to find her, and I planned to see her again.

As I passed my sister's shop, I banged on the window and stuck my tongue out at her, scaring some of her customers and their furry companions. She screamed "hoodlum" at me, but I pretended not to hear as I continued on.

I thought about going straight to my truck and getting to the gym, but I wanted to see her. When I stepped into Union Jack's, the hostess perked up, staring a little too hard at me. Her appreciation of me could be used to my advantage.

"Hi, how many?"

I smiled at her. "One in Hope's section, please."

Her posture dropped, and she lost the vibrancy she'd shown when I entered. "Hope's not in today."

"Do you know when she's working next?"

She shook her head. "I'm not allowed to say."

I leaned forward, giving her a good view of my arms. "What's your name?"

"Adriane."

"Adriane." Her name rolled off my tongue, and she shuddered, giving the effect I wanted. "Adriane, it would mean a lot to me if you told me when she'll be back. I promise I won't tell anyone you told me. She was a really good waitress, and my friend and I were a bunch of drunk asses the other day. I wanted to apologize."

She blinked at me. "Oh. Well…" She looked down at a piece of paper. "Looks like she's scheduled tomorrow."

I smiled and took her hand in mine. "Thank you."

"Y-you're welcome."

I walked through the restaurant and out the back door to the parking lot and my awaiting truck. As I headed off, I formed a plan. Dex was right, as much as I hated to admit it—I had to fuck Hope, and soon. Only after, with a clear head, could I take her on a date. That was if she said yes.

I'd given up trying to figure out what was wrong with me, and gave in to the devil in me that wanted her flesh.

When I walked into the gym with a smile on my face, I felt good. The emotion swiftly vanished when I saw our receptionist and scheduler, Dawn, leaning over the front desk and whispering frantically with Aaron, our youngest trainer.

My neck tensed and my jaw clenched as I walked forward. Something was wrong. Dawn's eyes widened when she looked up and saw me.

"H-hi, boss."

I looked between her and Aaron—who looked so nervous he'd turned white.

"What is it?"

"Well, Monica had me come in today for a few clients."

Dawn bit her bottom lip. "Andrew, Ashley, and Teri."

I turned my neck, my whole body tensing up, my fingers curling up to a fist. "Those are my clients." They both nodded, and Aaron turned pale. "Is she here?"

Dawn shook her head. "She's off today."

"Then she just caught a break, didn't she?"

Aaron leaned forward. "Jared, I swear I didn't have anything to do with it."

I held my hand out to him, and he slipped his in mine for a shake. "You're good, man. Calm down."

"If he'd been Shone…" Dawn trailed off.

I nodded. "That's a different story." I reached out for the week's schedule. It was all marked up, many spots with my name crossed off. The following day was the boxing class, and I tapped my finger over the event.

"Dawn, I hired you, and you've been a great employee. That being said, I have to ask you where your allegiance lies."

She wasted no time responding. "Monica talks down to me like I'm a fucking incompetent toddler. She's always telling me I need to lose weight because I represent the gym."

Aaron's eyes snapped to her figure, and he slowly looked up and down the length of her body. Kid had it bad for her.

I stared at her and shook my head. Dawn was petite, five-two and maybe weighed 110 pounds soaking wet. She was healthy and looked good. Her brown hair and brown eyes added to the girl-next-door look she had going on. Many of our female clients saw her and wanted to look like her. They didn't want to be like Monica.

I let out a strained breath. "Don't lose a damn pound. You look great, and it's obvious Monica and I no longer see eye to eye on what this gym represents." She smiled at me and played with the zipper on her hoodie. I turned to Aaron next. "How about you?"

"I know I'm still a newbie and all, but you took me under your wing. I've seen the underhanded shit she's done to you." He held out his fist. "I'm all yours."

I bumped his offered fist and nodded. "Okay, good." I looked back down at that damn boxing class. "Do you have the list of people signed up for the Thursday class?"

Dawn nodded. "Yeah. There are six people, and most of them are new members."

"Call them all up and tell them it's been cancelled for Thursday and moved to tonight." I looked to Aaron. "You up to teach a class?"

"Me?"

"Yeah. You've been taking my class and helping me for months. Plus, I've been watching you with your clients. Time for the next level. Besides, it's a small class—you'll do great."

"Thanks."

"I'll be able to help out if you need me, and we can talk this afternoon if you need any tips." I looked back to the schedule. Dex would be in later, along with Alexa. She'd had more than one blowout with Monica in the past, so I knew she would be on my side. By some luck, Monica's followers were all off for the afternoon as most of their clients were in the morning.

"We'll be good today, but not a word can be said to Candice, Jordan, Mike, or Stacie." They both nodded. I looked up at the clock above their heads. It was almost noon, and Andrew wouldn't be in for about an hour. "I've got to do some things in the office."

I flipped the schedule around and pushed it toward Dawn before walking around the desk.

"Boss?" Dawn stopped me, and I turned back to her. "I know it's been rough for you lately, and I'm pretty sure you've been thinking about your future here. If you leave, will you take me with you? I like working for you, but I'd have to quit if you left and Monica took complete control."

Her words gave me a pick-me-up, and I smiled at her. "Deal."

"Me, too!"

I rolled my eyes as Aaron raised his hand. "Back to work."

I closed the office door behind me and collapsed into my chair. It felt great to have the support of my employees, and Dawn's admission along with the support of some of my other employees had me thinking more and more about opening a place on my own.

The gym may have been Monica's idea, but it'd been my skill that got it off the ground and gave it four successful years. With us no longer together, our working relationship had gone from strained to bad. Our business was suffering because of it and had become a sinking ship in my mind.

Dex had a large client base that Monica was shifting to Shone, and her degrading remarks to Dawn pissed me off. Dawn was the one to find and set up our scheduling software. She kept us a well-oiled machine. Alexa was not only a trainer but a nutritionist as well, and she and Monica did not mix well. Add in an eager Aaron, who was great with every member I'd seen him come in contact with, and they made for a great team.

I flipped through my contacts and pulled up the numbers for my lawyer, and my friend, Dave, who was a commercial real estate agent. It wasn't the right time for it, but it was the necessary time to get things moving. For my own mental health, I needed to separate from Monica completely.

Chapter 5

Aaron did a great job teaching the beginner's boxing class. So well, in fact, a few of his students signed up for personal training with him. He seemed so excited.

The call with my lawyer went well, and he started the paperwork to separate me from Title Fitness. Luckily, we'd been talked into a Partnership Agreement when we opened up, something I was very thankful for as it was going to make what would've been a messy separation so much easier. However, I wasn't happy when he told me it would take about ninety days for everything to settle and that he needed to meet with both of us.

In other words, I needed to get a new place *very* soon. There was bound to be a shit storm when Monica found out I planned on opening my own place with half our employees.

We had signed a five-year lease, and there were only ten months left on the contract. She could hop along by herself in that time.

For the first time in months, I felt pretty good, and nothing was going to knock me down—not even Monica's persistent phone calls. My phone rang again on the drive to the gym, and for the fifth time in a row, I hit ignore. I knew she was pissed about the cancelled class. Two could play her little game.

As soon as I walked through the door, she was on me. "What did you do?"

"Why, sweet cheeks, whatever do you mean?"

Her face dropped at my condescending tone. I wasn't the beaten-down man she saw a few days ago. I'd come back with a vengeance and a devilish streak.

"You're a fucking asshole."

"And you're a fucking bitch."

Her anger surged. "I set that class up for Shone."

"Who doesn't know shit about boxing. He knows what little he learned in my classes and the few attempts by you." I leaned forward and glared at her. "He's a gym rat, not a trainer."

"He's a great trainer." Her jaw jutted forward.

I arched a brow at her and turned to Shone, folding my arms across my chest. "Where's the sartorius muscle located?"

He gave me a blank stare. "Umm." He looked to Monica for help. "It's in the forearm, right here." He gestured near his elbow.

"That's the supinator or five other muscles in that area. The sartorius is the longest muscle on the body." I drew a line with my finger down and around my thigh, then ended at the inside of my knee. "I figured it'd be pretty easy one to remember." I shook my head and looked back at Monica. "Why'd you hire him?"

Her whole body tensed, vibrating from the force. "Shut up!"

"Shut up? That's a terrible reason."

She screeched and stomped off to our office, slamming the door. Objects crashed against the wall, breaking, and I was happy I'd gone through and taken any personal items and personal information home the prior day.

Dex walked up, complete shock written on his face. "Dude, what happened to you?"

I shrugged. "I gave in."

"Gave in?"

"Gave up fighting everything. I'm going to have Hope and get Monica out of my life for good."

"Have you talked to Hope? Did you fuck her?"

"No, but she works tonight."

Dex slapped me on the back. "Good to see you again."

I swung my arm to the side and punched his stomach. "Back to work."

He rubbed his stomach and smiled. "Aye, aye, Capitano!"

I leaned against the front desk, smiling at Dawn. "Who's on my hit list today?"

She reached out and gave me a high five. "Welcome back, boss." She beamed at me. Was I really that far gone lately? "You've got Jason at two, followed by Sarah at three."

I nodded. "Plenty of time for a workout. Thanks." I patted the desk as I stepped away. "Yo, Dex!" His head popped up. "Workout?"

He gave me the thumbs-up and I moved to the locker room, a bit of a skip in my step that I didn't even realize I'd been missing.

Cassie and her husband were keeping Mom company for the night, so I was in no rush to get home after my last client. It wasn't a family dinner—those took place on Sundays—so I knew I wasn't expected to be there.

I had someone to visit.

Still clad in my workout gear and my black t-shirt with the word "TRAINER" written across the back, I drove back to Union Jack's to see the girl who made me crazy.

The hostess, Adriane, remembered me from the day before and sat me in Hope's nearly empty section. I vibrated just knowing she was near. When she came out from behind the kitchen door, I trembled and adjusted my hardening cock.

She stopped a few feet from the table and stared at me. "What are you doing here?"

I had to bite my tongue to keep from moaning at the view of her cleavage in her tank top. A ripple moved through every nerve in my body.

"I can't have dinner and a drink?" I quirked my brow at her. Her movements were slow and cautious as she closed the last few feet. "Why are you acting so afraid of me?"

She slammed a napkin down on the table in front of me and glared. "What can I get you to drink?"

I smirked at her. "I'm not sure I can have what I want."

She looked away, the buzzing heat between us increasing. "Dos Equis?"

I was pleasantly surprised that she remembered. "Water will do me for now."

She backed up, nearly tripping on her own feet as she turned to head to the bar, an embarrassed blush flooding her face. She looked over at me a couple of times, and I stared straight at her. Last time, I was unprepared to see her again, but tonight, I was going to make sure she knew I wasn't afraid of the intensity between us.

When she returned with my water and set the glass down, it slipped, tipping over and sloshing water onto the table. We both reached for it, and I barely managed to keep from touching her. The static current was still through the roof with how close we got. I couldn't imagine how bad it would be when I actually got some skin-on-skin contact.

"Sorry." She wiped away the spilled liquid with some napkins.

"Nothing to be sorry about, Hope."

Her eyes fluttered as I said her name, eliciting the response I was going for. The muscles in her jaw tensed.

"Are you ready to order?"

"I'd like the spicy veggie wrap."

"For your side?"

"Chips are fine."

I handed her the menu, and she started to go, then stopped. "Why?"

I sighed, knowing exactly what she meant—the same thing I'd given up on asking. "Fuck if I know."

She headed back into the kitchen, and I was left with a nearly empty area, nothing good on TV, and a water. Maybe I should've gotten the beer. Then again, the calories alone from the other night equated to about ten extra hours of cardio for my week. As much as I loved their pizza, I couldn't handle it twice in one week.

I pulled out my phone, distracting myself from thoughts of touching her, of letting my cock loose on her. Anything to keep me in check. Puppies seemed like a nice, safe subject.

"Fuck."

My eye twitched, recognizing the voice of my vapid ex immediately.

"Really, Jared? You didn't ruin things enough today, so you had to fuck up my dinner tonight?"

The hostess sat them directly across the empty space from me. Shone walked in behind her, ever the lost puppy.

"I was here first. Ignore me, and both our dinners will remain intact." I glared at her, hoping my death ray beams would work, but they were fresh out of laser gas.

Unfortunately, Hope was their waitress as well. I hated that she was subjected to their poison. As she placed a napkin on their table, it fluttered to the ground. Without thought, she turned around and leaned over, giving me full view of her fuckable tits.

I groaned and palmed my cock, pressing against the hard-on coming back like it'd never gone down when Monica entered the room. The sight killed me and ended way too soon, so I focused on her round ass and fucktastic curvy hips.

Yeah, maybe not such a good idea with the hell-bitch so close.

Once she got their drink order, she came back to check on me. "Refill?"

I licked my lips. "I can't stop thinking about what I really want."

She reached out and grabbed my glass. "And for now, that means water."

I leaned out of the booth to watch her ass as she walked away. No reason to be shy about it.

"A chubby girl, Jared? Really?" the evil voice called out from across the room.

"She's not chubby." I turned to glare at her, teeth grinding together.

She flipped her hair over her shoulder. "She's packing on a few extra pounds."

I swiveled in the booth to face her. "Are you saying that because you're a super-skinny, muscle-obsessed bitch, you can't see the beauty and sexiness in a soft, healthy, curvy body? I remember back when we met—when you were human—you weren't too far off from her."

"I was never that bad."

"No, you were never that *good*. She's a fucking goddess." I smirked at her and grabbed my dick. "Are you jealous that she can turn me on just by looking at her?"

Her gaze narrowed. "Shouldn't you be home with your mommy?"

"Shouldn't you be shutting your fucking trap before you piss me off any more?" I turned to Shone, who sat there with stupid written all over his face, staring at us. "Dude, her pussy isn't worth the hassle—I should know."

Monica jumped up, hissing, her face red and angry. "You wouldn't know good pussy if it jumped on your dick."

I remained staring at Shone, ignore her tantrum. "And how the fuck do you put up with her bitchitude? I mean, there's got to be tons of dim-witted girls out there that would be a perfect match for your color of crayon."

"Man, shut up. Stop pulling me into it." Shone shook his head and looked at her. "Babe, sit down and ignore him."

"You should listen to your pup."

"He's twenty-four, asshole!"

"And you're *thirty*."

"Shut the fuck up." She snarled at me, shaking, and by the expression on Shone's face, he had no idea.

"That's your comeback?" I quirked my brow at her and then tipped my head back, a strained laugh coming from my chest. "Thank God there are only ten months left on the lease."

And there it was—the first hint of what was going down. She'd find out next week anyway.

Her expression was priceless—wide-eyed horror. It shocked me to see, because she was smart. How could she not see the writing on the wall? We were done as business partners.

"You think I'm afraid of you?" Her hand shooed at me. "Crawl on back to your mommy's house."

I stood up and faced her full on, every muscle tight. I was ready to fucking hit her, and there was no one to hold me back or calm me down—though Shone stood, moving to stand between us.

"Say another fucking word about my mom, bitch."

"What? What will you do, dickwad?"

I'd become so lost in the blazing anger that I didn't notice the surge of lust that suddenly pumped through me. It wasn't until a scream echoed off the walls that my vision cleared and I saw Hope at their table.

"Oops," she said, picking up a now-empty cup of soda.

"You idiot!" Monica's screech could be heard blocks away.

"I'm sorry." Hope remained calm and collected, nothing like when she was near me. A glance my way with a small smile was all I needed to understand she'd done it on purpose.

It was the first sign she'd given me to show she was interested in me for more than the strange, overpowering attraction between us.

Chapter 6

The manager came out and asked us to either calm down or leave. There was no way in hell I was leaving, and Monica didn't back down either. Instead, in her soaking wet clothes, she finally stopped talking and sat back down. She and Shone stayed on their side and left me alone.

Peace at last.

Well, as close as I would get to peace with the fire that ripped through me every time Hope came back in the room. Serving more tables meant she swung by more, and the lust was compounded with each pass. All control was slipping fast from me—I wanted to tear her apart. My muscles flexed, begging to touch her, consume her and burn together. I wanted to take her on the floor right there in front of Monica.

"How's your wrap?" She tipped the water pitcher in her hand, refilling my glass.

I finished up my bite and stared into her blue eyes, another shiver running through me, cock twitching. "I didn't come here for the food, but the wrap is good."

Her hand tightened around the handle, lip caught between her teeth again as she shook her head. "Stop."

I grabbed hold of the pitcher, afraid of what I would do if I touched her skin. "I wouldn't even if I could."

She gave me one last look before turning and walking away. Something inside me got angry every time she left, but at the same time, I loved to watch her body move. Each stride of her long legs begged me to follow.

After she refilled my water and I paid the bill, I figured I'd worn out my welcome for the day, especially by the glares I got from the manager. There was always tomorrow. As I exited the bathroom, ready to jump into my car, her melodic voice filled my ears.

"Mac, I'm going to take a break. Table two has their check."

She walked past the restroom alcove and out the back door. My cock twitched as I stood there, deciding what to do. Truth be told, there was no decision. I'd already started following her.

I knew what I *wanted* to do, what I *needed*. The devil was winning again, because I was going to get it.

She'd reached the edge of the building by the time I got out the door, my pace even, measured, letting the thirst for her fill me. When I rounded the corner, she was leaning against the brick wall, looking down at her phone and typing away.

She shivered, her gaze lifting to me, lips parting. "What are you doing back here?"

I stopped a few feet in front of her. "Are you saying I can't be back here?"

Her gaze flitted around, trying not to look at me as she squeezed her phone. "No, but you should leave."

The nervousness radiating from her only fueled the energy moving in waves between us.

"I was walking to my car, but I felt you calling to me." I stepped forward and caged her with my arms. The vibration, the desire-filled excitement, skyrocketed.

So close.

Inches apart.

All sense was gone, replaced by a greedy hunger to touch her.

"You need to get away from me."

"Why? Because you can't control yourself?"

She reached out and pressed against my chest. A shudder rocked us both at the contact. Tiny, dick-twitching whimpers and a hitched breath had me moaning. The skin beneath her hand burned.

"Fuck you."

I smirked and leaned in closer to whisper in her ear. "I plan to."

"Oh, God." She tilted her head, exposing her neck, fingers clenching against my chest as she fisted my shirt and pulled me closer. The heat from her body was hotter than the fires of hell where I was sure to end up.

"He's obviously not here. I'm Jared." I couldn't get her to look at my face, but her breath had become labored. "You look fucking tasty in these little scraps of cloth. Tempting me. Are you trying to get a cock shoved up your tight little cunt?"

"It's my uniform."

I removed one hand from the wall and set it on her waist, groaning at the electric shock that burst through my body, firing off every cell in me. My fingers caressed her exposed flesh as I moved down to her hip.

"It's a tiny uniform. Does it get you a lot of offers?"

She nodded, and my hand flexed on her hip, all soft women curves, succulent beneath my touch.

Her other hand fisted into the fabric of my shirt at my waist. "I like to feel their eyes on me."

A small step forward, aided by her tugging grip, and the gap between us disappeared. My mouth dropped open, hips rocking my painfully hard cock into her stomach. "That's a dangerous game, little girl."

Her breath was hot against my neck. "I get so wet thinking about some guy hard for me. Fantasize about being taken against a wall, hard and fast."

The skin on her neck pinked—I loved to see the flush of her skin. I leaned in closer, my lips ghosting against hers. "Is that what you want me to do?"

"Yes."

"Fuck," I growled out. My hand slipped around to the front of her shorts and cupped her pussy. "You're not a good girl, are you? Underneath your innocent façade, you're fucking naughty, is that it?"

She whimpered and pushed against my hand.

"How do you like to be punished? By my hand as it strikes against your plump backside? Or maybe by my cock slamming into you so hard you see stars? How about keeping you on edge, unable to come, until I let you?"

Her eyes were completely clouded over and heavy, her voice almost a whisper. "I don't care."

"You don't care?"

"As long as it means you're touching me."

"Only me?"

She nodded and pulled me tighter to her. "Only you make me feel this way."

I popped the button on her shorts and pushed my hand into the small gap, groaning at the heat of her bare, wet pussy.

"I told you I'd be back to take what's mine." My lips crashed to hers, taking what I'd dreamed of for days.

The euphoric sound of her moans traveled between us, pushing me to kiss her harder as her arms wrapped around my neck, her nails digging in. My fingers slipped between her pussy lips and inside. She drew in a ragged breath, her hips flexing forward, pushing me deeper.

I rocked them in and out, my palm pressed against her clit. High-pitched whimpers moved from her mouth to mine and shot through my cock, forcing me to move. Shallow thrusts against her relieved some need while her tongue sucked on mine and her nails dug into my skin. She almost had me coming in my shorts.

I wanted to get her off, watch her come undone from my hand, before I shot off.

"So fucking soft and tight. My cock can't wait."

An unknown voice called out for her from around the corner, and I groaned.

"Fuck!"

She whimpered, pressing harder against my hand, rocking faster.

"Back to work, little girl. You have customers that need servicing."

I pulled my fingers out and looked into her eyes as I stuck them in my mouth. Fuck, she tasted good, and I groaned, lapping up all of her. She let out a strangled cry, her head against the brick, lids heavy as her hips rolled, thighs clenching together. Neither of us was going to get off right then.

So close. I had her on the edge.

I stepped back and adjusted my near-bursting hard-on. She licked her lips, her gaze locked on my bulging tent. I grabbed hold of it, making sure she knew what waited for her.

"We're not done."

She licked her lips. "Fuck, it's big."

I smirked at her. "It's what you have to look forward to."

Her boss called out for her again, and without breaking eye contact with me, she called back. "Coming!"

"Almost, but you will." Instead, she'd have to suffer through work turned on and wanting my cock.

I hated watching her walk away, but loved that she looked back before disappearing.

A heavy breath left me, and I leaned against the brick exterior for a moment to calm myself. It didn't help, so I pulled my keys out and headed to my truck. The second I got in and closed the door, I reached in my shorts and pulled my cock out.

"Fuck!" *My poor cock.*

The head was purple and stiff to the max, leaking a trail of pre-come. I moved my fingers along the underside, hissing when I hit the extremely sensitive edge. It would only take a few swipes like that for me to explode. It still amazed me that I hadn't when I'd been pressed against her with her lips on mine.

~ 46 ~

I stuck my fingers in my mouth, tasting any last bits of her that remained while I stroked my cock. Every muscle tensed, built up from hours of frustration in her presence. My mouth dropped open, hard breaths coming out before a hard shudder rocked my body and my cock began firing off.

I looked down to watch each spurt land on my black shirt, wishing it was all over her skin or deep inside her pussy. That was where it needed to be.

Chapter 7

When I arrived home, I found Mom asleep on the couch, the TV on some home show, which reminded me I needed to mow the grass in the morning. As I entered my room, I threw my shirt into an overloaded laundry basket. I pursed my lips and sighed, walking over to it and picking it up, then headed down the hall to my mom's room. With both her basket and mine in hand, I made my way down two flights of stairs to the basement.

I'd neglected the house chores over the last few days, thanks to whatever had taken control of me. There was no denying it—I wasn't myself. The emotions boiling inside me shook my mind from my depression, but the lusted-out beast who craved a woman beyond sanity? He freaked me out.

After starting up a load, I headed back up the stairs. Cassie had cleaned up the kitchen before she left, reminding me my sister rocked. I walked into the den and sat down at the desk, sighing as I moved the mouse to wake up the computer. I picked up a stack of mail and flipped through it.

I threw medical bills to the side as I pored through everything else. I loved the ones with big bold letters

"Patricia Lynch, you're a winner!" Very important mail. I made sure to tear it up and toss it into the trash.

I stretched my neck out and logged on to the computer. The first thing I did was check my mom's accounts, and I didn't like the number I saw.

"Shit." Her insurance couldn't keep up with the costs of her treatments, especially with her being on unpaid medical leave. Between my dad's hospital stay and now her illness, there wasn't much money left. I logged on to my own account and hit the transfer button. I'd built up a nice savings in preparation to buy a house with Monica, and now it was going to help ease my mom's financial stress.

"Jared?"

Looking over my shoulder, I saw Mom standing in the doorway. "Nice nap?"

She slumped down in the sofa chair and wrapped a blanket around her shoulders. "Cassie put me in a food coma."

My lip quirked up. She was eating—a good sign. "How're you feeling?"

"Tired." She sighed and looked over at the desk. "What are you doing?"

"Paying the bills."

She pursed her lips. "Thank you." Her head tilted as she looked at me. "There's something different about you this week."

I nodded. "Yeah."

Silence stretched between us.

"You going to tell me, or do I have to play twenty questions?"

I rubbed my face and lifted my arms up in a stretch. "It's…complicated." I sighed. "I met someone."

She perked up, a smile forming on her face as she sat a little straighter. "And? Tell me about her."

My face heated up. There was no way I could tell my *mother* about what had been going through my mind.

"Her name is Hope, and she's pinup-girl gorgeous."

Her eyes widened. "Pinup? That's different. What else?"

I blew out a breath. "She works at Union Jack's, and visits St. Joan of Arc."

"And? You're killing me here, Jared."

I grimaced. "It's because that's all I've got. The truth is, I don't know much about her, but we have this uncontrollable attraction."

She arched her drawn on eyebrow. "Condoms are your friend."

"Mom!" I stared at her in stunned disbelief.

"What? Do you want to have a child with a woman you just met?"

I held my hands up. "Who said I didn't want to get to know her?"

She leaned back. "Why haven't you yet?"

I sighed and shook my head. It wasn't something I wanted to tell my mother, but now that she knew about Hope, she wasn't going to let up. "Because every time I'm near her, all I can think about—all I can feel—is intense lust." My jaw clenched, hands flexing into fists. "And it *controls* me."

She nodded, staring at me for a moment. "Have you asked her out?"

"Not yet."

"Well, don't be an asshole."

"Mom!"

"You keep saying my name like that." She chuckled. "I'm not stupid. Plus, you're over thirty now, and you lived with a woman for five years. I know you are very familiar with sex and how it works."

I rubbed my face again and shook my head. "You're not supposed to be so casual about it."

She shrugged. "You're an adult."

"It's just weird."

"You think that means I'm going to continue to sugar-coat things for you?"

"No, it'll just take some getting used to."

"Oh, I almost forgot to tell you. Cassie's having a girl."

I beamed at her. "Yeah? That's awesome."

For some reason, it was that bit of news that made it hit home—I was going to be an uncle. My little sister was going to be a mom. I was going to be uncle to a little girl and bound to spoil her rotten.

She nodded. "Now, you're the oldest—where's your contribution?"

My mouth dropped open. "Who just told me to make sure I use a condom?"

She shrugged. "What can I say? I want grandbabies."

"Unbelievable. Why didn't you ever say anything before?"

"I liked Monica in the beginning, but she was very self-centered and turned out to be a lying, cheating whore. She wouldn't have been a good mother."

I leaned back in shock. Amazing how the truth came out from those close to you on how they felt about your girlfriend once the relationship was over. "Tell me how you really feel."

"She used you." She leaned back and settled into the chair, a mischievous smile spreading on her face. "Have I ever told you how your father and I met?"

I nodded and sat back as well, wondering where she was headed. "At a party in college."

"That was where, but not the how."

My brow scrunched. "Okay."

"My sophomore year, my friend Beth took me to a party. From the moment I walked in, my skin crawled. Not in a bad way, but it tingled."

I knew exactly what she meant—I'd experienced it at a growing rate for days.

"We made it into the kitchen, and my eyes locked on a gorgeous set of blue eyes, then *bam*!" Her eyes were bright before softening.

"I remember Dad saying he got caught in that moment." The memory was a fond one, my father describing the emotion that came over him. When I was a kid, it was like a fairy tale for boys as he explained to me that cooties weren't such a bad thing.

"There's a lot he didn't tell you. But I have to ask— did you ever feel anything like that, what you do with this girl, with Monica?"

I shook my head. "There was attraction, just like with every girl I dated before her."

Mom was more animated during our conversation than I'd seen her in weeks or months. "That right there tells me there could be so much more with this girl."

"Why?"

"Because half an hour after I entered the door to that house, I was in the bathroom having sex with your father, and I didn't even know his name."

My jaw dropped open. "Wait, what?"

"And his girlfriend of a year had come to the party with him."

"Holy shit! Seriously?"

She chuckled. "No, but that's the way I always thought it would've gone if he hadn't been in a relationship."

I blew out a hard breath. She was trying to kill me. "What *did* happen then?"

"He avoided me all night. At some point, I'd gone to use the restroom, and when I came out, he was walking down the hall. It was narrow, and being a gentleman, he gave me the right of way. Before I made it past him, his arm flew in front of me. The struggle was evident even as he caged me with his arms against the wall. I wanted him to kiss me, desperately wanted it. I thought I'd die if he didn't." She touched her lips with the tips of her fingers, almost like she could still feel it. "He was so close I felt the heat of his skin, the zinging spark between us."

"How did he stop?" I'd become enraptured by the story, because I knew the struggle she was talking about.

She sighed. "Someone called his name, and he woke from his trance. He was so angry with me after that."

"Why was he angry with you?"

"Well, he later admitted it wasn't me, but himself. Two days after the hallway incident, he broke up with his girlfriend, and he blamed me for it. He had his whole future with that girl laid out—he planned to propose. When he saw me, everything changed."

"Wait, I missed something. He broke up with the girl he planned to marry two days later?"

She nodded. "You know your father was a good man. It was love at first sight, though he didn't want to believe it. Having those feelings for someone other than her, he knew then it wasn't right with her. For weeks we bumped into each other on campus, and he became even more upset with each encounter. He said he couldn't seem to get away from me."

"How did that make you feel? I mean, what was going through your head?"

"It was an attraction on a level I only ever experienced with him. It was confusing, because I thought about him all the time—the worst crush ever. Three weeks after the party, in the middle of the night, he showed up at my sorority house. Three months later, you were conceived."

"That was fast."

She shrugged. "There's a reason I wanted you to know all this. Times might not have always been easy, and though we knew we were soul mates, we were also human and fought. If any of what I've described is the feeling you get with this girl, don't let anything stop you."

I shook my head. "It was not love at first sight in my case."

"How can you be so certain?"

"Because it's lust. I'm not thinking with anything other than my…" I trailed off, almost blushing. The conversation was definitely out of the norm.

"And what happens when you catch your prey?"

"We'll have sex."

"And then?"

I threw my hands up into the air. Why was I talking about Hope with my mother? "I have no idea."

She smirked. "Fifty bucks says you won't be able to let her go." I side-eyed her, and the smirk grew into a grin. "You don't want to take that bet, do you?"

I sighed and rubbed my face. No, I didn't want to take that bet, because deep down I knew having her once would never be enough.

Chapter 8

The next morning, I awoke with another raging hard dick. I stared at it and the tent it made in my sheet before reaching in and grabbing it. The sting of Hope's touch still lingered, along with the feel of her lips and body pressed against mine. My mind conjured up images of her from the night before, fueling my fantasy.

A few quick tugs later, I exploded all over my stomach. One down, but I had a feeling it was the first of many for the day.

After I showered and dressed, I headed down to find Mom. She sat in her chair, eating something and watching the morning news. I contemplated making a big protein-rich breakfast, but opted for a protein bar and some of the juice I made the previous day.

I sat down on the couch and opened up my breakfast. "Take your meds, eat your breakfast, and when I get back, we'll head out."

Her brow scrunched as she looked at me. "Where are you going?"

"I'm just running down to St. Joan of Arc for a bit."

She quirked a brow at me, a smirk forming on her lips. "Okay."

I finished off my bar and juice, then kissed the top of her head. "I'll be back soon."

As I walked down the street, I buzzed with excitement. It was the official one-week anniversary since I first laid eyes on Hope. My plan was simple—have a talk with God. Then I would pray Hope stopped by on the same day every week.

When I walked in, a man sat near the front, but the rest of the church was empty. I didn't let that deter me and slipped into a pew. I folded my hands in front of me and bowed my head.

"Well, big man, you found a way to get me here again." I snickered as I looked to the altar. "As you know, a lot has changed for me this week. I can't figure out if that's you answering my prayers or giving me new challenges, but I feel more up for it."

The old man at the end got up and walked slowly down the aisle and past me. A quick look around told me I was the only one there. The sun came out from behind the clouds and shined through the stained glass windows, bouncing color around.

"Mom's doing better the last few days, and I found out I'm going to have a little niece. Can you take the cancer away so she can have time with her granddaughter? Please." Tears began clouding my vision, and I swallowed hard. "She's all Cassie and I have." I wiped away the wetness and took a steadying breath. "Okay, Cass has Darren, but you know what I mean."

The emptiness that had been missing for days washed over me again. I leaned forward and rested my head on my arms against the pew in front of me. The ache in my chest was crippling. When I thought I was going to burst, a tingling sensation moved down my spine and spread through my body.

I sat up and looked around, but there was nothing, no sound. Turning back around, I sighed and looked back up at the altar.

"I have to know...am I possessed? Whenever she's near, I become some monster with only lust on the brain. Every part of me wants to devour her, touch every part of her body with mine. Repenting won't do anything for me, because I want her, and I can't stop even if I tried. Is that why you put her in my path?"

Again, nothing.

I got lost in my thoughts and stared. After a few minutes, I snapped out of it and prepared to leave.

"Oh, and one last thing. Please give me the strength to resist bitch-slapping my ex, because she really deserves it. And let me get through the dissolution of our partnership without too much drama. I'd appreciate it."

As I stood, the tingling burst into a full flame, and I fell back into the pew. It wasn't my imagination or some phantom sensation. Hope had to be here.

Footsteps bounced around the walls, and my body came alive with each one. They slowed for a moment, but I didn't turn to look at her. The pace picked back up, and she took a seat in the pew across the aisle from me.

My whole body tensed, muscles flexing. I turned a little bit to look at her. Her eyes were closed, fingers clasped together, head bowed. I shouldn't have looked at her, because once I did, I was transfixed and couldn't look away. What was in her prayers?

My gaze moved down her profile, and my dick took note that she wore a skirt. When I looked back up, she was peeking over at me. I stood up and walked the few steps that separated us, then slid in next to her.

Being inches from her was painful. My cock screamed at me to touch her—lower her down to the bench, pull up her skirt, and plow right into her. I reached up and pushed the strand of hair blocking the view of her beautiful face behind her ear. The expression on her face made me groan—so innocent and so inviting.

Her gaze moved back down, and the full lips that I wanted nothing more than to have on me in any way, were moving, but I couldn't hear anything. With hands still folded in her lap, I realized she was praying. Being so close, I ran the back of my fingers against her soft, pink cheek. The current became too much, and she trembled.

With a small "Amen," she looked up and turned toward me.

Her eyes held me captive, and I ran a thumb across her full bottom lip. "Why are you here? What sins do you need to be absolved from?"

She blushed and glanced at the ground. "Why do you come here?"

I wanted to tell her I come for her, not for church.

"I asked you first. Why do you *come*?"

She stared at me for a moment, her tongue running against her lips, wetting them. "Forgiveness for the sexual thoughts that run rampant through my mind. I think the Devil is playing with me. His fires burn me from within."

I swallowed hard, forcing my hands to keep still. After such a confession, I wanted to turn the heat up on her fire.

"Why are you here?"

I thought on it for a moment. There were many reasons. "Hope and guidance, and recently, forgiveness for my desire to corrupt what appears to be an innocent soul with sexual deviancy."

She nodded. "The Devil has you as well."

"A deadly sin has me—*lust*. It makes me a devil possessed with the desire for a woman's body to be wrapped around mine. *You* have me."

She smiled. "Then Hope has you."

"I need Hope in my life." My voice was low.

Her eyes widened. "You shouldn't say things you don't mean."

I pushed her down onto the bench and trapped her body with mine, then crashed my lips to hers. My whole body shook, hands gripped tight at her waist. Her mouth was sweet, and I wanted to taste every inch.

"Oh, I know *exactly* what I mean. *I want you.*"

"Jared."

My fingers dug in as the blood thrummed almost violently through me. The airy, wild way she said my name shot straight to my dick, rocking my whole body on the way down.

I nipped her bottom lip. "Say it again."

Her fingers tangled in my hair, pulling me down to her as she arched up, eyes locked with mine. "Jared."

I reached down and grabbed her thigh, pulling it up and spreading her legs to get between them. With a thrust of my hips, my covered cock pressed against the warm heat of her pussy. I groaned and took her lips as my arms pulled her closer.

Making out became dry humping in seconds. Her hands clawed at me, her body trying to meld with mine.

I reached between us and popped open my jeans. I needed her, was desperate for her.

The loud clang of the church door closing echoed around, and we froze. After a quick pause to listen, my head popped up over the back of the pew. There was no one to be seen, but the faint clack of more than one set of footsteps on the stairs alerted me to people being near.

Looking back down at Hope made me groan and press into her.

"Fuck, baby."

Her eyes were heavy and dark, and her fingers played with the waist of my jeans, pulling me to her. I took hold of her hands and lifted her up, wrapping them around my neck until she was standing. When she stood on her tippy toes to kiss me, I didn't have to lean down as far to close the half-foot height gap between us.

"Come on. Let's find somewhere a little more private." Fuck, I was going to explode if I didn't get inside her now.

I scanned the huge room, looking for some place to hide away. There was always the bathroom, but my gaze landed on the ornate, carved dark wood of the confessional booth. I took her hand and yanked her down the aisle and into the confined space of the small confessional box. As soon as we were in, I sat in the chair and pulled her down so she was straddling my lap. My hand grabbed behind her neck and brought her lips down to mine.

I wasted no time running my hand along the inside of her thigh and against the part of her that'd been torturing me for days. The heat that radiated off her pussy was intense. I slipped my fingers under the edge of her panties. Her folds were slick, wet with her arousal, and I moaned into her mouth.

"I need in you, now."

Her hips rocked against my dick, driving me mad. I kissed down her neck, sucking her skin in, biting and marking her as I got my cock out.

I pushed her hips down, impaling her with my cock. She drew in a hard, sharp breath that turned into a stuttering, guttural moan. The sound, combined with her tight, wet walls squeezing me, was overwhelming. I groaned, my eyes rolling back, head resting against the confessional chair.

Fucking perfection.

The fires of hell felt heavenly with her wrapped around me.

"Ride me, baby," I whispered against her skin.

I dug my fingers into her hips and guided her up and down my cock. My grip moved around to her ass, forcing her down as I thrust up. Little moans and whimpers came from her open mouth as she bounced on me.

Every feeling was too much. I didn't know if I was going to go insane or not before I came. I picked up the pace—harder, faster, pull, thrust. The booth shook around us, her pussy clamped down on me, and she threw her head back in a silent scream.

The pulsing waves of her walls milked me, and I wanted to give it what it asked for.

"Are you on birth control?" A little late to ask, but her answer would make a big difference.

She nodded, uttering a barely audible "yes" as she continued to move up and down on my cock, still shaking from her orgasm.

"Good, because I'm going to fill your pussy up."

My muscles were flexing and tight, my cock harder than it'd ever been. My thighs were burning, tired, and my balls were high. The pressure was too much, and I let go, roaring as I pulled her down hard and pushed up, burying my cock all the way in. Jizz shot out and into her—exactly where it needed to be.

She fell against me as we relaxed, and her head nestled in the crook of my neck. Neither of us moved as we caught our breath. I kissed down her neck, licking and nipping the whole way, tasting her as my hand moved up and down her back. She felt so perfect in my arms.

"I'm not done. I want more. Can we go to your place?"

She shook her head against my neck. "My roommate is home." I cursed, wishing she lived alone. "We can go to your place."

I laughed, my dick not liking the lack of privacy. I wanted to take my time and consume her.

"I'm living with my mom right now." My eyes widened, and I moved my arm to look at my watch. "Shit. I have to go."

She froze, her face dropping. "Oh. Okay." Everything about her became stiff. She started to get up, but I pulled her back down and to my chest, pressing my lips to hers. She sighed and melted against me.

"My mom has an appointment with her oncologist."

She blinked at me and nodded slowly in understanding. "Is she okay?"

"Not right now."

She trailed kisses down my neck, and I nuzzled hers. Somehow she knew I didn't want to talk about it but needed comfort at the same time.

A few minutes passed, and I helped her straighten her clothes out before stuffing my dick back in my jeans. When she was done throwing her hair back into a ponytail, I opened the door, the old hinges creaking loud and reverberating around.

Hope slid out, then me, and I ran right into her back. She'd stopped just outside the booth. Multiple sets of eyes stared at us, including one of the priest's.

I smiled and nodded to them, then grabbed her hand and walked out.

"Well, guess I'm not going back there," I said as we ran down the steps.

Her cheeks were bright red, hand over her mouth in horror. "That was the priest who did my Confirmation!"

I pulled her close and pressed my lips to hers. "That's a bit mortifying. Especially because you weren't all that quiet."

She swatted my chest. "Yeah, well, you're the one who made me make those noises."

I grinned. "Oh, I know, and I plan on doing it again. So, when are you free this week?"

She eyed me suspiciously. "Why?"

"Because I really want to see you again. And as soon as possible. Like tonight."

She smiled and looked down at the sidewalk. Fuck, she was cute when embarrassed. Her eyes widened, and her mouth popped open as she looked down.

"Oh, no…" Her legs snapped closed, thighs clenching.

I groaned and grabbed her ass. "Fuck, baby, is my jizz slipping out and down your thigh?"

"Yes." She whimpered.

"Good." I smirked at her, my hand still in hers as we walked to her car. "I've marked you as mine."

Chapter 9

Mom was right—one time wasn't enough. Having Hope only made my cravings for her worse. Compression shorts became a constant part of my daily wardrobe—I had to contain the beast somehow.

Especially when she walked into my gym unannounced.

I groaned as I stared hypnotized at her sexy hips swaying as she walked my way. She smiled at me and wrapped her arms around my waist, not caring that I was sweaty. I pressed my lips to hers, nipping at her bottom lip.

"Excuse me."

I pulled back and sighed, looking over at Teri, who had her arms crossed and was huffing in annoyance.

Hope waved at her. "I'm just going to lean on your pole." She motioned over to the support beam a few feet away.

I smirked, unable to resist. "You can lean on my pole anytime."

Her mouth dropped open, and I couldn't stop from laughing.

It'd been two days since we defiled the church. Even though we hadn't gone on a date, one was in the works. Until then, neither of us could stay away for too long, which was one reason she was in the middle of the gym.

It also happened that my client, Teri, was her roommate.

"Oh, come on! This is my hour." Teri smacked my chest with a gloved hand. "You two can fuck later." She pointed to me. "But stay away from the kitchen! I spent an hour bleaching it this morning."

My devilish laugh came out, and I turned back in time to see her face drop. She was in for it. "Oh, you're in trouble now. Blitz!" Usually Teri punched ten to each side before switching, then taking a break, but she was going to hurt for that comment. "Again."

She glared as me and muttered "fucker" under her breath.

"Come on. Push it! Harder!"

She pummeled the sparring mitts until her arms had little fight and she gasped for air.

"Okay, break." I tossed the mitts on the floor and reached forward, removing one glove before pulling on the other.

Hope handed Teri a water bottle, and she attempted to drink between hard breaths. A few rounds later, we were done. Hope was still leaning on the pole, and as soon as Teri went off to the locker room, I closed the gap, pressing my body against hers. I pushed her into the pole as I wrapped my arms around both, trapping her.

"Hi," I said, smirking at her and pressing my cock into her stomach.

She nabbed her bottom lip in the fuck-sexy way she always did. Her being coy drove me and my cock insane. "Hi."

"Come here often?"

She rolled her eyes and fought a smile. "My boyfriend works here."

I quirked a brow at her. "Boyfriend?" We hadn't really talked titles… Well, we really hadn't talked—mostly fucked—but we were getting there.

"Boyfriend." She was firm in her word choice and gave me a little attitude with it. "Got a problem with it?"

I shook my head. "No, but, baby, let me be your boyfriend. I own the place." And soon I would fully own a place, without Monica.

"Own the place? Well, then, you have an enticing proposition."

I leaned in and kissed her neck, humming against her skin. "How about I offer up another enticing proposition?"

"All right, break it up." Teri tapped her foot next to us. "Come on, Hope, we have to get to class."

She looked to Teri and then back to me, a small pout on her lips. "Sorry."

I groaned and gave Teri the evil eye.

"Don't look at me like that, you devil."

I bent down and gave Hope a last kiss. "I'll see you tonight."

She nabbed her lip and looked at me from under her lashes. "Maybe I can act out one of my fantasies."

I smirked and pulled her closer. "What's that, my naughty girl?"

Her lips were close to my ear, tickling the hairs on the back of my neck. "I want to *service* my customer."

I groaned and squeezed her ass. She pulled away, blowing me a kiss before turning to catch up with Teri.

I knew the Devil and lust were in us both.

But if I was going to hell, the trip would be worth it with Hope by my side.

About K.I. Lynn

K.I. Lynn spent her life in the arts, everything from music to painting and ceramics, then to writing. Characters have always run around in her head, acting out their stories, but it wasn't until later in life she would put them to pen. It would turn out to be the one thing she was really passionate about.

Since she began posting stories online, she's garnered acclaim for her diverse stories and hard hitting writing style. Two stories and characters are never the same, her brain moving through different ideas faster than she can write them down as it also plots its quest for world domination…or cheese. Whichever is easier to obtain… Usually it's cheese.

Visit my website www.KILynnAuthor.com
Follow me on Twitter @KI_Lynn_

www.ingramcontent.com/pod-product-compliance
Lightning Source LLC
Chambersburg PA
CBHW070646130626
46555CB00006B/2733